# Mitzi's World

Seek and Discover More Than 150 Details
in 15 Works of Folk Art

Text by **Deborah Raffin**
Paintings by **Jane Wooster Scott**

ABRAMS BOOKS FOR YOUNG READERS   NEW YORK

# Winter is here . . .
## soooo cold . . . oh, dear . . .

# Cold Snowflakes

*Can you find . . .*

ONE broom, a bell (ring-a-ding-ding, things to sell),

a church, a scale, a shovel, 4 small red birds,

a bookstore, 9 boots, a blue-and-white horse blanket,

and teeny-weeny, itsy-bitsy, ditzy Mitzi?

# Cold City Streets

*Can you find...*

TWO tower needles, a striped coat (worn by a man holding a note), a tree guard, a moon, a fire hydrant, a cash register, 9 hanging magazines, 2 blue crates, 3 skylights, and teeny-weeny, itsy-bitsy, ditzy Mitzi?

# Cold Moonlight

*Can you find...*

THREE hearts, a chocolate cake (fun to bake), 4 round
wheels, a star cookie, a wood-burning stove, 2 candy canes,
3 cupcakes, 8 white windows, a snowman, and teeny-weeny,
itsy-bitsy, ditzy Mitzi?

# Cold Tracks

Can you find...

FOUR bright streetlamps, a buggy (pulled by a horse, of course), 2 American flags, 6 children, a train engineer, 10 pine trees, 6 farm silos, a groundhog, 3 yellow coal cars, and teeny-weeny, itsy-bitsy, ditzy Mitzi?

# It's spring . . .
## soooo warm . . . let's sing . . .

---

# Warm Friends

---

*Can you find . . .*

FIVE round-shaped trees, a blue umbrella (next to
the flower fella), 3 seagulls, a bridge, 4 sailboats,
a blue garage door, a skateboard, 2 joggers, a stone chimney,
and teeny-weeny, itsy-bitsy, ditzy Mitzi?

# Warm Community

*Can you find...*

SIX musicians, 3 people (floating up, up, and away,
just for the day), 2 green bows, a banjo, a monkey,
48 balloons, a giraffe, a tricycle with a basket in the rear,
6 slices of watermelon, and teeny-weeny, itsy-bitsy,
ditzy Mitzi?

# Warm, Furry Companions

*Can you find . . .*

SEVEN black leashes, a party hat (pointed . . . rat-a-tat-tat),

a schoolhouse bell, a white kitty, 6 red leashes, a trophy,

3 men wearing bow ties, 13 dogs, 4 blue ribbons,

and teeny-weeny, itsy-bitsy, ditzy Mitzi?

# Warm Wheeling

*Can you find . . .*

EIGHT cycles on the town path, an ice-cream cone
(one scoop . . . all alone), 5 white caps, 4 steps, a woman
with a ponytail, a purple dress with 2 red stripes,
a waterwheel, a red door, and teeny-weeny, itsy-bitsy,
ditzy Mitzi?

# Summer is here...
## soooo hot... let's cheer...

—

# Hot Contestants

—

*Can you find...*

NINE flags forming the shape of a kite, cotton candy (pink and dandy), 5 seagulls, a life preserver, a carousel horse, a sand castle, a beach ball, a ping-pong table, 3 red buckets, and teeny-weeny, itsy-bitsy, ditzy Mitzi?

# Hot Breezes

*Can you find....*

TEN large flags flapping on a single pole, a red polka-dotted shirt (just cleaned, no dirt), 11 sailboats with sails aflutter, a Space Needle, a mountain, 2 yellow city buildings, 2 rowboats, 4 tires, 7 flower pots, and teeny-weeny, itsy-bitsy, ditzy Mitzi?

# Hot Balloons

*Can you find . . .*

ELEVEN letters that spell "Far Rockaway," a clock (round . . . tick-tock), 2 jukeboxes, 3 kites, 2 bags of popcorn, a yellow star, a car, 4 green lights, hot dogs for sale, and teeny-weeny, itsy-bitsy, ditzy Mitzi?

# It's fall …
# soooo chilly … have a ball ….

## Chilly Noses

*Can you find …*

TWELVE letters that spell "Veterinarian," a skunk
(who stunk—whoo!), a banana, a snake, a ball, a canary,
2 goldfish, a red heart, a lamb, and teeny-weeny,
itsy-bitsy, ditzy Mitzi?

# Chilly Pumpkins

*Can you find…*

THIRTEEN letters that spell "The Produce Hut," a scale
(next to the cider for sale), 18 wheels, 4 pumpkins,
a blue pitcher, 5 cows, 20 geese, 2 barrels with red apples,
a candle, and teeny-weeny, itsy-bitsy, ditzy Mitzi?

# Chilly Art Lovers

*Can you find . . .*

FOURTEEN windows trimmed in white and gray,

a weather vane (a cat who sat), 3 cars, 2 lamps, a windmill,

9 paintings, a child pulling a sled, a running boy,

a covered bridge, and teeny-weeny, itsy-bitsy, ditzy Mitzi?

# Chilly Hustle and Bustle

Can you find....

FIFTEEN cents for oxtail stew, an apron (white and tight),
a yellow bowl, a red-and-white-striped pole, 7 hanging
magazines, 3 blue lights, 2 knives, a scooter, 2 pairs of red
suspenders, and teeny-weeny, itsy-bitsy, ditzy Mitzi?

*And now another new year begins.*
*Where will Mitzi appear next?*

# Folk Art

Paintings, sculptures, textiles, or objects created by artists from around the world to share their cultures.

## A Few Styles of Folk Art

1. Naïve art: Extremely simple work by *untrained* artists (such as people who didn't study art)

2. Neo-naïve art: Also extremely simple work, but created by *trained* artists

3. Environmental art: Large pieces constructed outdoors

4. Outsider art: Work that is very unusual and different from what most artists are creating during the same period, and sometimes hard to understand

5. Memory art: Work that depicts life in the past

## Which styles do you think were used to create ditzy Mitzi's World?

ANSWER: Neo-naïve art / Memory art

The illustrations in this book are oil paint on canvas.

For my family, who are a constant source of love and challenge—Vernon, Tira, Ashley, George, Oliver, Preston, Audrey, and Charlotte

—J.W.S.

For my cutie-pie Taylor-Rose, the joy of my life

—D.R.

Library of Congress Cataloging-in-Publication Data

Raffin, Deborah.
Mitzi's world / by Deborah Raffin ; illustrated by Jane Wooster Scott.
p. cm.
ISBN 978-0-8109-8004-4 (harry n. abrams, inc.)
1. Picture puzzles—Juvenile literature. 2. Dogs—Juvenile literature.
I. Scott, Jane Wooster, ill. II. Title.

GV1507.P47R35 2009
793.73—dc22
2008049720

Text copyright © 2009 Deborah Raffin
Illustrations copyright © 2009 Jane Wooster Scott
Book design by Maria T. Middleton

Printed and bound in China
10 9 8 7 6 5 4 3 2 1

Abrams Books for Young Readers are available at special discounts when purchased in quantity for premiums and promotions as well as fundraising or educational use. Special editions can also be created to specification. For details, contact specialmarkets@hnabooks.com or the address below.

HNA
harry n. abrams, inc.
a subsidiary of La Martinière Groupe

115 West 18th Street
New York, NY 10011
www.hnabooks.com